THE GOSPEL OF

MARTIN LUTHER KING, JR.,

TO

THE SOUTHERN BAPTIST

THEOLOGICAL SEMINARY

Jeff Hood

The Gospel of Martin Luther King, Jr., to the Southern Baptist Theological Seminary

Second edition

Jeff Hood

Barber's Son Press

York, Pennsylvania

Published by

BARBER'S SON PRESS

York, Pennsylvania

Library of Congress Control Number: 2020941378.

ISBN Number: 978-1-7347188-1-2.

Barber's Son Press Publication #4.

Second edition.

10   9   8   7   6   5   4   3   2   1

TABLE OF CONTENTS

Midrashical Note

This book tells the remarkable story of the Rev. Dr. Martin Luther King's invited appearance at Southern Baptist Theological Seminary in Louisville, Kentucky. We will read about how the invitation happened, what the events were like, and what happened behind the scenes of the public presentations.

What we experience in this book is an angle on the life and Ministry of King, as an African American rights activist, as a Christian, as clergy, as scholar, as a reconciler, as a provocative healer, as a radical. As such, King was in every sense of the word a public theologian, and in this story we will witness him entering the civic, academic, and religious settings seamlessly and simultaneously.

We will also hear the story of how the lure of the Holy Spirit called individuals into bold and prophetic movements—even if just for a moment.

This story is self-aware of the danger that such legends pose to white-wash history, knowing well how such legends about Martin Luther King, Jr., are employed to suffocate the exigency of King's presence and ministry. Rather, we celebrate moments of convergence and sparks of hope birthed in the tensegrity of difficult conversations and actions.

Dr. Hood has assembled numerous first-hand accounts to create a narrative. It is not necessarily a scholarly exercise. It is, rather, a religious practice of hagiography—that is, the celebration and storied recollection of stories of saints—

ultimately in honor of the God who speaks through the mess that is the church.

The words of King in this narrative are presented in red letters. Of course, the book is tipping a pious nod to "red letter editions" of the Christian Bible. But beyond this it is a religious expression of God speaking truth to power with a subversively gentle fire of the Spirit.

It is an expression of the Word proclaimed.

The presentation of *The Gospel of Martin Luther King, Jr., to the Southern Baptist Theological Seminary* should be encountered with these motivations and understandings in mind, positioning our spirit to—after the words of Dr. King—

> **"accept finite disappointment,
> but never lose infinite hope."**

C. D. Rodkey
Publisher

INTRODUCTION

Stories matter.

Every witness brought me closer.

Faith was swift with every word.

I'm so glad I didn't listen to the academic experts. Their rules would have killed this moment.

The heart wasn't created to be enslaved like that.

In fact, I believe that zealous citations have destroyed history... or at least the practice of it. Each little number seems to be a stake into the art of storytelling...the apocryphal experience. I'm not interested in inerrancy.

I'm interested in the story.

I'm interested in truth.

I'm interested in that day.

Beauty can never be bottled up... and such an incarnation can't either. God was with them... of that... there is no doubt.

Memory has painted a portrait of profound revelation.

 Listen and you will be redeemed.

Rev. Dr. Jeff Hood
January 19, 2019

BEGINNING

The incarnation descended.

The story of these moments is the story of the souls that breathed them.

In the creation...

PREPARATION

There was nothing out of the ordinary. The meeting was going to be boring as shit. Nobody wanted to be there. The collective subconscious moan was to get it over with as quickly and as painlessly as possible. The Gay Lectures were coming up and the committee had some invitations to extend.

"Only slightly interesting..."

Maintaining the historical monotony of it all was the present task of the gathered—

> Chairman Dr. Allen Graves, Dean of the School of Religious Education;
>
> Dr. Nolan P. Howington, Professor of Christian Ethics;
>
> Dr. Wayne Ward, Professor of New Testament;
>
> Dr. James Leo Garrett Jr., Professor of Theology;
>
> Dr. Willis Bennett, Professor of Christian Ethics;
>
> and Dr. Henlee Barnette, Professor of Christian Ethics.

"However you want to describe what was going on...we were just ready to get the hell out of there."

"We knew that these speakers would say nothing to excite anyone. Our boring meeting would prepare the way for boring lectures."

Papers started rustling. Bags started zipping. Everybody was ready to go.

"Not so fast, guys!"

"Why don't we invite Dr. Martin Luther King, Jr., of Atlanta?"

Nobody said a word. The censored words they would normally say were doubly censored.

Sensing an opportunity to slightly move beyond their present situation, the group supported the recommendation.

Bodies sprang from their seats and everybody quickly left. The names were then to be sent to the seminary president, Duke McCall.

The first warning shot came later that night.

Graves called McCall in an excited panic. The reply was measured at best.

"I was very skeptical at first. You have to understand how big of a gap there was between the pro-segregationist lay people that made up the majority of the Southern Baptist Convention and our racially progressive faculty. Plus, I'd only been there for about ten years at this point. I also wasn't the initial choice of our more progressive faculty members. I don't think I was scared."

Detractors saw him as a denomination man. Throughout his tenure, he tried to be something else.

"I knew the invitation was important to them...and I didn't want to let them down."

On the other hand, racists and their churches funded Southern Seminary.

"I was in an unenviable position, to put it mildly."

"The entire faculty was to meet in a few weeks. What use was there to hurry?"

The faculty wanted to issue the invitation and just move on.

McCall wasn't having it.

"I wanted them to know what they were getting into."

Looking everybody dead in the eye, McCall leaned in:

"Boys, it's your call, but realize this is going to cost us somewhere between two hundred and five hundred thousand dollars!"

"Money well spent!"

The room bust out in laughter. The vote was unanimous.

Terrified, McCall begged:

"Please don't talk about this until I can figure out how to deal with it. This is no affirmation of political views! Do you understand me? This is about hearing a good preacher and that's it! Do you understand me?"

Can you imagine what it was like for Dr. King to open that invitation? The most racist denomination in the country was inviting him to speak. King relayed his surprise to anybody who would listen.

Slowly, surprise turned into excitement at the opportunity.

"There was no way in the world that he was going to miss this show."

The King was coming.

Racial tensions were on the rise.

"Convention politics were white hot...and that was before I told anybody that King was coming."

Such ignorance wouldn't remain for long. Calls and letters started to flood the seminary.

"I grew more nervous by the second. As President, you can't imagine the stress that I was under."

McCall couldn't keep this one under wraps. One after another, cancelations came in.

"From students to professors to preachers to laypeople to funders to anybody with a pulse... nobody wanted to be associated with Dr. King or us."

In spite of it all, they all hung tight.

"I guess we were steadfast or stupid in going down together."

Desperate to blunt some of the tension, McCall started making calls to less than reputable helpers. While the White Citizen's Council of Kentucky was not the Ku Klux Klan, they certainly were no friends of Jesus. To offset the heat, McCall decided to invite one of their vicious racists to speak at the seminary.

"I'm not proud of that invitation...but I did what I felt like I had to do."

Raybun Sugg wasn't your average racist...he was the president of the whole damn council... the piece of shit of pieces of shit.

"We were beyond embarrassed that McCall pulled that stunt. What in the hell did he think he was going to accomplish?"

The sermon—if you could even call it that—took place days before King's.

"He basically tried to convince us that God was a racist. It didn't work."

Right or wrong, nobody responded cordially. People just wanted to get the hell out of there.

"As faculty, we were beholden to progress alone...this type of cheap pacification was McCall's job. We refused to allow ourselves to be tainted by it."

Emmanuel McCall was particularly incensed.

"I felt so betrayed. I was the only black student at the school at the time. Can you imagine? Many students just viewed it as entertainment. I was not interested in being a part of no minstrel show."

Black suits were everywhere.

"I was afraid. I didn't know who they were. I just knew that they meant business."

The secrecy of it all only heightened tensions.

"Rumors were being manufactured by the second."

"These men are here to keep us safe."

Most of the campus didn't believe him. Raybun Sugg had already killed President Duke McCall's credibility.

"We didn't know about King's visit until it was right up on us. I never doubted that the community would be nice to him. I was more worried about outsiders coming in."

"I was unaware of any controversy. I had too much else to do. Although—I can assure you—I wouldn't have missed it for the world."

"You need to remember that King was famous then... but certainly not the widely known figure he is now."

Nobody had any idea of what was coming.

Graves couldn't get out of the room. People accosted him from every direction. Pastors demanded to know about King's visit.

"Is it true? You better hope not!"

Graves waffled. Graves ducked. Graves ran. Immediately, Graves called Garrett.

"This thing is white hot. Is King even worth it?"

"We can't rescind it now. McCall will smooth it over. Just enjoy the ride, brother."

Louisville was exploding.

The integration of public accommodations kept being delayed...and the patience of students had expired.

Just a few days before King arrived, the first arrests of a massive campaign of civil disobedience took place. The jail filled up quickly. There was no going back. It seemed that the entire city was joining.

City leaders just couldn't figure it out. How do you create middle ground between racists and activists?

—*You don't.*

The seminary population was energized and their participation in the struggle was increasingly amplified.

Organizing trips downtown to protest, Garland Offut—the first black student at the seminary—led the way.

"God was on fire in those days."

The world was changing.

"Jesus was coming in on a white horse!"

"We were ready for whatever came next. God had brought us to this moment. We sure as hell weren't turning back."

The administration didn't know what to do.

"Tensions were hot as hell."

McCall felt he couldn't turn back. Regardless of his fear, the King was coming.

In fact, the plane had already arrived.

ARRIVAL

Word spread like wildfire.

Many found it highly upsetting.

Some were prepared to do something about it.

Local media covered every minute of it.

There was no going back.

Graves met King at the bottom of the plane, ushering him directly into an awaiting limousine. Though frightened, law enforcement was everywhere, and they were instructed not to leave King's side until he left.

Amid of all of the excitement, Graves leaned over and informed King that McCall had unfortunately been called away and would be unable to join them.

"Unbelievable."

King was nervous. Nobody seemed to care.

"We were just trying to get him there in one piece."

When they pulled up to the front of the school, it was like the triumphant entry. Professors and students rushed the car.

"This is remarkable!"

"I am well aware."

Ward recalled a very different Dr. King than history has remembered.

"He was very quiet...very nervous...and very unsure as to how to interact with us."

The group thinned down to just professors.

"We were trying not to overwhelm him."

Upon arrival to the office, Dr. King graciously received a signed copy of Barnett's *Introduction to Christian Ethics*, generously replying,

"I've already read it, and I hope men like you are the future of the Southern Baptists."

The group of men couldn't get enough. Picture after picture. Signature after signature. Question after question.

"I guess we hogged him a bit."

Regardless, the hour had arrived.

King was nervous. No amount of prayer was going to change that. The organ blast jolted him.

On the way out of the office, protestors rushed the side door.

One of the messages stuck with him:

"Go to hell!"

Feeling like he had to keep going, King waded through all the white folk.

It didn't matter how many times he was told things were fine... he was ready to get it over with.

"I was frightened for him."

E. McCall recalled the place being absolutely packed.

"I didn't know the vast majority of people there. I think that's what scared me the most."

It didn't matter how anyone felt, the show was about to begin.

INTRODUCTIONS

"Howington puffed him up pretty damn good."

"Our speaker has achieved a place of significance far beyond most, if not all, in this room and certainly beyond most men of his age.

"He is a native of Atlanta, Georgia, born on January 15, 1929 (the year of the stock market crash). He has been at the center of the crash ever since.

"He is a well-educated and well-trained man, fully equipped for the task that providence has given him.

"Dr. Martin Luther King, Jr., has been tagged as the American Gandhi, a modern Thoreau, the Moses of his people, the premier prophet of social justice of our time and quite a few names far less complimentary than these.

"Like Moses, he elected to identify himself closely with his people in the Deep South, following his educational pilgrimage to the northeast.

"He has never failed to live out his commitments to non-violence and serves as an example to us all.

"He is a Baptist, a true American, a Christian gentleman, a man of God, and while he has drawn inspiration from many sources he unashamedly follows the Christ in whose name he now comes to us.

"He is a King who has humbled himself and truly learned how to be a tremendous servant to America.

Turning around, facing Dr. King directliy, Dr. Howington continued.

"I speak for the administration, faculty and students of The Southern Baptist Theological Seminary when I tell you that we are overwhelmed and honored to have you in our midst.

"Gentleman… *The Rev. Dr. Martin Luther King, Jr.*"

"We all knew something magical was upon us."

ADDRESS

The words didn't flow. Nothing did.

The King on the tape is not the great orator King. Clearly, he was deeply nervous. Rows upon row of white folk sat in judgment of his every word.

As King desperately searched for his rhythm, he stumbled at least five times. King was still young, and it showed.

Regardless, it didn't take too long before he hit his stride.

"I am overwhelmed and honored to be a part of this chapel service. I have looked forward to this experience ever since I got the invitation.

"Surprisingly, this is not my first time in this chapel, I attended services here once before when you lent this space to the National Baptist Convention's Women's Auxiliary some years ago.

"As a result, I have suspected this seminary to be a place of racial thought quite different from the region that it serves for some time now and my interactions today have solidified such suspicion."

"He called us hope. It was bizarre."

"His title, 'The Church on the Frontier of Racial Tension,' was appropriate. He was clearly telling us that we were responsible for our own redemption."

"He respected us... when he didn't have to—and that got our attention."

"Our asses began to move to the edge of our pews."

"In those first lines, we began to hear the King."

With gusto, Dr. King spoke of the horrors that had occupied the black experience, reminding everyone that they had always been clothed in a false Jesus.

"We knew that we were responsible. Hell, our founders were all slave owners... our churches were full of some of the most racist people that you would ever meet. Our ears were open."

After an extended history lesson, King declared that now was the time to go beyond integration—*that* was too simple. Now, he said, was the time to open your heart. King was clearly preaching for a decision. The message was simple... follow me.

"Now we stand on the border of... a new order of freedom and equality... the old ideas *of segregation* have exhausted themselves and a massive evil resistance has arisen to new ideas...

"This is the crisis we see in America."

Such words could have never flowed at most Southern Baptist churches. They wouldn't have been ready for the truth. Violence would have been inevitable.

But things were different in the chapel.

Souls were moving. Truth was on fire. The challenge festered with every word.

"The church must indeed urge and demand that its worshippers develop a world perspective to the detriment of the blatant regionalism and nationalism that plagues so many of our churches... truly, all of life is inter-related...

"We are caught in a single garment network of mutuality, tied in a single garment of destiny..."

"There was absolutely no question that King was speaking directly to *us*... We were moved...How could you not be?"

"King didn't stop... in fact... he was just getting warmed up."

"Segregation is wrong, because it damages the soul of the Negro... the underlying philosophy of segregation is diametrically opposed to the underlying philosophy of Christianity."

This was the most direct challenge to the prevailing social order that had ever been uttered in that solemn space.

"King was clearly speaking against many Southern Baptists, but he was not saying things that professors, like Howington and Barnette, hadn't said before.

"*This* was different, though.

"This was a moment in which it started to become very real to so many of us—*for the very first time*—it was quite powerful."

The incarnation continued to flow in and out of the hearts of the gathered.

Dr. King challenged the gathered to speak the truth about intentions of the Negro.

> **"Many are worried about intermarriage...**
>
> **"I want all of you to make a commitment to me right now that you will go home and tell all your local church folk that are terrified of such things... the Negro just wants to be your brother, not your brother-in-law."**

These words garnered a huge roar of laughter. After a pause, King pushed on.

> **"The church must not only clarify ideas, but it must move to the realm of social reform."**

King pivoted seamlessly to the requirements of the economic teachings of Jesus:

"...so that others might live."

"Those economic zingers stung."

In the perplexity of the moment, King directly challenged the students to give themselves to the struggle.

Hearts were exploding all over the room. Everyone knew what was now required of them.

As everyone anxiously awaited for further instructions, King closed.

> "I call upon all men of good will to be maladjusted to the evils of this age... your churches, whether they know it or not, are in desperate need of your maladjustment.
>
> "Will you lead them?
>
> "No lie can live forever... Either we live together as brothers or perish together as fools...
>
> "Truly, now is the time to transform the evils of our southland into a beautiful symphony of peaceful relationships...then and only then will the sons of God be able together to shout for joy...
>
> "Go."

The gathered arose to their feet in jubilant affirmation.

King had just garnered the first recorded standing ovation in the 103-year-old history of the seminary... and the last one since.

"The world hasn't been the same since."

CENTER

Throngs of people rushed forward.

It was as if they wanted to make him their King at that very moment.

After pushing through the throngs of people, Dr. King accompanied Howington; Barnette; local pastor John Claypool; and photojournalist Frank Stanley, Jr.

The men immediately started to ask King questions.

"I was in absolute awe."

"Let's talk about the seminary."

"There are just so many more important concerns to talk about."

King reminded him...

"You must fight wherever... space is always a secondary concern..."

Stanley proceeded to ask about King's views on the integration campaign going on in the city.

"I'm for it."

Everybody got a good laugh at King's statement of the obvious.

"What I don't understand is why every single student at this school is not out there?"

None of the gathered had an answer.

Though the gathered did not want to let go, the conversation had to end. King was scheduled to speak to the combined ethics classes.

Along the way, King suggested the seminary begin to offer classes in social activism. The laboratory could be to participate in actions of nonviolent resistance.

"*Damn*, that sounds *amazing*!"

ETHICS

Hundreds packed the chapel to hear a work from the King.

King promised the students one hour of his time stating,

> "If I'm late for my next appointment, then it's God's will…"

Laughing, he continued.

> "I want this period to be your period. I'll speak briefly on my nonviolent philosophy and then try to answer all the questions you have, as we bind ourselves in a shared search for truth at this hour."

Most of the professors and students gathered were sympathetic to the cause, but their knowledge was limited.

King picked upon this very quickly.

> "There are three ways that oppressed people can deal with their plight.

> "First, they can acquiesce and resign themselves to their fate. This rarely accomplishes anything much less a guarantee of rights.

"Second, they can use violent physical force. The problem is that violence never brings about a permanent peace.

"The third way is the spiritual movement of non-violent resistance. This is a moral option for a moral people that recognizes the image of God, and its accompanying goodness, set deep inside even the nastiest of souls.

"Nonviolence seeks to touch this goodness and unite humanity in love as one."

King paused for a moment to let these words that marinate in their souls.

Then, the questions began.

"How do you justify breaking the law in various boycotts? Is it not violent to put people and their workers out of business?"

"I know, young man, that you want peace, but we as a people cannot secure our peace and rights without these means. We desire to bring justice, freedom, and human dignity into these businesses in order to make a better society for everyone."

"Don't you disrespect the law by calling for resistance?"

"Any unjust law that does not square with God's

law does not deserve to be followed or even
exist. Hitler followed the law. Did he not?"

"Can you conceive of a time when it will be expedient to
renounce the nonviolent method and turn to violence?"

"No, I cannot think of anytime when violence
will be necessary."

"How do we avoid becoming identified with extreme groups
like the White Citizen's Council, on one hand, and the
NAACP on the other?"

"Extremism is not always a bad thing, young
man. I pray that we all grow more strongly in our
extreme love of Jesus Christ. We should be
hungry to be known as extremists...

"Once again, being identified with extremism is
not a bad thing, one just must be extreme about
the right thing."

"What is your attitude toward Malcolm X and the Black
Muslim Movement?"

"We must continue to condemn the philosophy
of these movements and all of the major Negro
leaders do condemn the philosophy of Black
Nationalism generally. This movement is
divisive and dangerous."

"Doesn't a private business have the right to choose whom it serves?"

"No, a private business does not have the moral authority to deny someone service based on the color of their skin."

"The extended answers that King gave to these short questions truly wowed the students and converted many of them to a belief, not just in the aims of the Civil Rights Movement, but in the means he espoused as well."

Upon the completion of the last question, Barnette walked to the podium to end the session. In deep appreciation, the students rise to their feet to once more to give King a standing ovation...this one actually rowdier than the first.

As the crowd silenced, Barnette broke protocol and told the students that they were about to go downtown for a secret lunch meeting with Mayor Hoblitzell and the Board of Aldermen.

"Dr. King could really use your prayers as he seeks to offer advice on the peaceful integration of Louisville… we also have something else to offer you as well."

He then presented King with a petition demanding swift integration signed by most, if not all, of the faculty and students. The crowd was electrified.

"We were ready to storm the gates of hell."

Turning to Barnette, King declared:

"Nowhere have I been shown so much love by any educational institution... black or white, or purple for that matter."

LUNCH

Though they were running late, King didn't mind. It was as if he left part of his soul back at the school.

Before long, they appeared before the city leaders.

The mayor motioned King to come to the front of the room. Without delay, King presented the petition:

"We, the following faculty and students of The Southern Baptist Theological Seminary, located in Louisville, Kentucky, wish to express our deep concern about the speed by which true integration is occurring in the city, and lend our encouragement and actions to the integration of all establishments in the entire city of Louisville, recognizing the inalienable freedom of every person to patronize businesses, secure employment, secure housing, and express their God-given desires, loves, and talents."

Everyone was surprised. The seminary wasn't exactly known for getting involved.

"As I know these are thoughtful men of God, I will certainly meditate on these words."

King didn't eat a bite of his lunch... pushing for change was too important.

The professors watched in awe.

Upon the conclusion of many important conversations, King headed back to the school.

COFFEE

Upon arrival, King declared victory.

"They didn't have a choice but to listen!"

"King came in, sat down, and the gathered faculty all made their way around him. Then he began to talk and were all just in awe of the man. You have to realize: this man was truly a prophet and most of us had never met a prophet before."

"In different dialects... with different sounds... with different words... the question was recycled over and over again... 'What more can we do?'"

"Get out of your classrooms and into to the street. Show your folk just how courageous you can be. Show them that you won't back down.

"Show them that justice is inevitable.

"As true followers of Christ, you are the witnesses they need to show them the way. Now is the time for boldness."

Nobody wanted to miss anything.

"There was a holiness in the space."

The Dean got excited.

"Dr. King, you moved the congregation with your message today in a way I have never seen a preacher move people before. You are unbelievably gifted.

"So... would you consider accepting a distinguished position in our homiletics department?"

"Nobody could believe he did it. None of us thought old Penrose had it in him."

"Dr. St. Amant, I am so deeply honored by your offer. I could never in my wildest dreams have expected to entertain such thoughts, but like Nehemiah of old, I am doing a great work and I cannot come down. I am a man under divine orders for as long as I have breath."

"I, for one, breathed a sigh of relief at his response. We were all very progressive and our people, obviously, were not. They usually left us alone if we didn't make too much commotion, but if King had accepted that offer, we would have reaped the whirlwind."

Shortly thereafter, King left for his last speaking engagement. Before departing, King briefly turned around and said,

"You have truly given me hope, that because of you and your efforts, the Southern Baptist Convention will one day be a home to all of God's children."

"Wow!"

RALLY

When King arrived at Quinn Chapel African Methodist Episcopal Church, he was greeted by thousands of cheering students.

With determination, King climbed into the pulpit.

"I have this day experienced a tremendous outpouring of love and appreciation from the students and faculty of The Southern Baptist Theological Seminary. As some of you might know, this is the flagship seminary of the often racist and segregated Southern Baptist Convention.

"Be encouraged, there are many white brothers and sisters associated with that school who are going to change the hearts of white folks, church by church.

"Such events encourage my heart, beloved. It gives me hope that segregation is as dead as a doornail, and the only uncertain thing is the day it will be buried.

"Keep fighting, for the time is drawing short.

"As for these sit-ins you all are conducting, this is not just a lot of noise over a hamburger.

"Negros aren't hungry.

"This is a demand for respect. Tame your egos and humble yourselves to forgive the white people who have hurt you. Draw upon the spirit of Christ and never surrender to injustice.

"May all that I have seen today in Louisville proceed forth as an example to the rest of the South."

The crowd erupted. In that moment of euphoria, King utilized the prayer of an old slave preacher:

"Lord, we ain't what we ought to be.

Lord, we ain't what we want to be.

Lord, we ain't what we are gonna be.

But, thank God, we ain't where we wuz."

The prayer perfectly described all that he had met.

END

Late in the evening, Dr. King boarded a late-night plane for Atlanta. He left behind pinholes of light in the darkness of the night.

"Amen."

The ascension was complete.

Surely, the King is coming quickly.

SOURCES

Audio

King Folder: The Southern Baptist Theological Seminary Archives: April 11, 1961 Audio Recordings of Martin Luther King Jr.'s addresses in chapel and in the combined ethics classes.

Barnett Collection: Wake Forest University Library: Audio Interviews that Henlee Barnette did with Allen Graves, Leo Garrett, Wayne Ward, and Nolan Howington.

Interviews

January 15, 2008: Interview with Rev. Charles Worthy (now deceased), pastor and student during the King visit.

January 22, 2010: Interview with Dr. Emmanuel McCall, the only black student at Southern Baptist Theological Seminary during the King visit.

January 25, 2010: Interview with Dr. Wayne Ward, Professor of New Testament at Southern Baptist Theological Seminary during the King visit.

January 25, 2010: Interview with Dr. Glenn Hinson, Professor of Church History at Southern Baptist Theological Seminary during the King visit.

February 1, 2010: Interview with Dr. James Leo Garrett, Professor of Systematic Theology at Southern Baptist Theological Seminary during the King visit.

February 8, 2010: Interview with Dr. Duke McCall, President of the Southern Baptist Theological Seminary during the King visit.

February 16, 2010: Interview with Dr. Leroy Seat, Retired Southern Baptist Missionary, student at Southern Baptist Theological Seminary during the King visit.

Henlee Barnette: Interview in Southern Baptist Theological Seminary Collection.

Archives

The Southern Baptist Theological Seminary Library.

The Henlee Barnett Papers at Wake Forest University.

The Southern Baptist Historical Library and Archives in Nashville, Tennessee.

AUTHOR

The Rev. Dr. Jeff Hood is a Baptist pastor, public theologian, and activist living and working in the hills of Appalachia. The author of over 30 books, Dr. Hood's work has appeared extensively in the media, including the *Dallas Morning News, Fort Worth Star Telegram, Atlanta Journal Constitution, Los Angeles Times, WIRED* magazine, and in television news from ABC, NBC, CBS, CNN, MSNBC, Fox News, NPR, and others. Dr. Hood is a radical mystic and prophetic voice to our closed society.

Among his many books:

The Collected Sermons of Jim Jones (ed.)

The Courage to Be Queer

The Execution of God

Frances: An Interpretation of the Gospel of Luke

Jesus on Death Row

Last Words from Texas

The Queer

The Queering of an American Evangelical

The Rearing of an American Evangelical

Barber's Son Press

York, Pennsylvania

www.ingramcontent.com/pod-product-compliance
Lightning Source LLC
Chambersburg PA
CBHW070609180626
46817CB00005B/2060